Duck Cakes
For Sale

For Ann, with love,
remembering the ducks.

J. L.

For Carol.

K. L.

A Meadow Mouse Paperback
Douglas & McIntyre
585 Bloor Street West
Toronto, Ontario M6G 1K5

Canadian Cataloguing in Publication Data

Lunn, Janet
Duck cakes for sale

"A Meadow Mouse paperback".
ISBN 0-88899-157-6

I. LaFave, Kim.   II. Title.

PS8573.U55D83 1992   jC813'.54   C91-095447-X
PZ7.L85Du 1992

Design by Michael Solomon
Printed and bound in Hong Kong by
Everbest Printing Co. Ltd.

Duck Cakes
For Sale

BY Janet Lunn
PICTURES BY Kim LaFave

A MEADOW MOUSE PAPERBACK

Groundwood/Douglas & McIntyre

Toronto/Vancouver

There was once an old woman who left the city to get away from all the noise and confusion. Out in the country she found a small house by a creek with a big shade tree in the back yard.

"This is just right for me," she said, and she settled all her favorite old things in her new house. Then she sat down to admire the view from her window.

"The creek looks lonely," she thought. "I'll get a duck to swim there."

And off she went to see the farmer who lived down the road.

"Have you got a duck I could have?" she asked.

"A duck? Lady, you're lucky. I've got two." The farmer gave her two downy yellow ducklings.

Every day the old woman fed grain to her
ducklings. In time they grew big. Their down became
feathers. They made a nest by the back step.

One morning there was a big green egg in it.
In a few days there were six more eggs. In a few
weeks the eggs were hatched into a new family of
ducklings.

The ducklings grew up. Soon there were more eggs. Then there were more ducklings, then more eggs, then more ducks, then more and more and MORE until the whole back yard was full of ducks. They were quacking and scolding. They were splashing in the creek. They were tramping in each other's way. They were making more noise and confusion than there had ever been in the city.

"There's no room here for me!" cried the old woman. At once she began to gather in the eggs so no more could hatch.

But there were too many eggs for one old woman to eat. So she made pancakes and lemon butter. Soon her tables were piled high with pancakes, and her shelves were crammed with jars of lemon butter.

She made custards and cookies, omelets and puddings, quiches and yorkshires. She made deviled eggs, pickled eggs, creamed eggs, scotch eggs and egg salad sandwiches. Every ledge and lampshade was covered with the egg dishes the old woman had made.

Still there were eggs, eggs and more eggs. Every
day. And out in the yard there were ducks and
more ducks in the trees, in the bushes, squabbling
on the steps and quarreling in the creek.
    The old woman had an idea. She made a sign.

DUCK CAKES FOR SALE
Ducks, drakes
Custard and cakes
And lots of other things
(even feathers)

Before long a car stopped, and a man and woman came to the door for custard and cakes.

"Would you like some tea, too?" the old woman asked.

"Yes please," they said, and when they left they took enough feathers to stuff two pillows.

The man and woman told all their friends in the city about the tea. Their friends came and brought their friends, and soon it seemed everyone in the city was coming to the country for custard and cakes.

The back yard was full of ducks. The front yard was full of people. Cars were lined up way down the road.

There were more people in the living room having tea, and the kitchen was full of pancakes, lemon butter, custards, cookies, omelets and puddings, quiches and yorkshires, deviled eggs, pickled eggs, creamed eggs, scotch eggs and egg salad sandwiches. Bits of green eggshell were everywhere.

The old woman threw up her hands. "Help!" she cried. "What am I going to do? I've never seen so much noise and confusion in all my life!"

At that moment two old ducks pushed their way into the house. They looked the company over slowly and carefully. Then they turned and waddled back outside. They quacked two loud QUACKS. They lifted their wings and flew off into the evening sky.

One by one, the other ducks followed after.

In a few days, when the eggs were all gone and the people had stopped coming for tea, the old woman set everything to rights. Then she sat back in her chair and looked out at the view.

"I wonder," she said to herself as she rocked back and forth, "if it might be nice to have one red hen."